Stacie Maslyn has written over 20 stories for children. She and her husband, Darren, live in Mission Viejo, California, with their four children.

Jane Schettle is a part-time illustrator and graphic designer, full-time wife and mother of two, and church youth group leader who lives in Oshkosh, Wisconsin.

Mad Maddie Maxwell
Text Copyright © 2000 by Stacie K. B. Maslyn
Illustrations © 2000 by Jane Schettle
Requests for information should be addressed to:

Zonderkidz™
The children's group of Zondervan
Grand Rapids, Michigan 49530
www.zonderkidz.com

Zonderkidz is a trademark of Zondervan

ISBN: 0-310-23207-4

Cover and interior design by Cynthia Tobey

Printed in China

01 02 03 04 05 /v DC/ 10 9 8 7 6 5 4 3

Mad Maddie Maxwell

Written by Stacie K. B. Maslyn
Illustrated by Jane Schettle

Zonderkidz

Maddie Joy Maxwell
charged from her room,
Her face filled with fury,
her voice filled with doom.

"Where is it?

Where is it?

Oh, where on earth is it?

My jump rope is missing!"

she boomed.

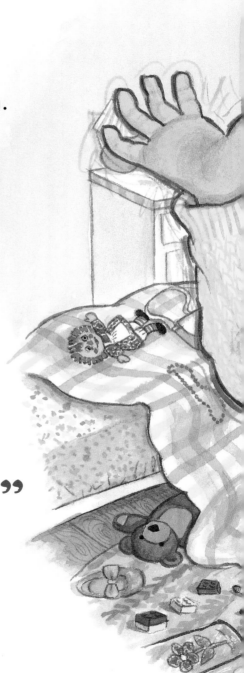

She raced to her sister with wild, angry eyes.
She caught little Julie quite by surprise.
Without any shame
Maddie gave her the blame.
And she hollered in poor Julie's face.

She sprinted past Julie.

"Get out
    of my way.

I can't stop
to talk;

I can't
    stop to play.

My jump rope
is missing.

Good-bye
and good day!"

At the pond with his pole, she caught brother Seth.
She was red-faced and panting and quite out of breath.
She thought that he'd hoped to catch fish with her rope.
She knew that she'd found it at last.

"Seth, YOU took my jump rope from under my bed!"

"Who, me?"
"Yes, YOU."
"Not me."

"Then who?"
"Missy?"

She stormed by old Seth.

"Get out
of my way.

I can't stop
to talk;

I can't
stop to play.

My jump rope
is missing.

Good-bye
and good day!"

Missy, her big sister,
so that's how it was!
Maddie knew now for sure
that she had it because
that's how big sisters were.
(Of that she was sure).
So she charged
all the way back home.

"Missy, YOU took my jump rope from under my bed!"

"Who, me?"
"Yes, YOU."
"Not me."

"Then who?"

Missy got up from the chair where she sat.

"Where are you going?"

Maddie angrily spat.

"Maybe…," said Missy to her very mad sissy, "you still need to look a bit harder."

Missy walked over to Maddie's white bed.
She bent down to look and she lifted the spread.
"It's dark and it's dusty.
You won't find it. Trust me!"
Maddie knew they were wasting their time.

Missy pulled out
three or four magazines,
a doll, a board game,
and two pairs of jeans,
a crumpled-up dress,
and a whole bunch of mess.
Then she reached to the
darkest back corner.

"It just **isn't** there, old Miss Smarty Pants!

Where is it?"

Maddie shouted.

"I gave you **your** chance!"

But just as she said it,
she came to regret it,
as Missy pulled out
her jump rope.

It was there all along, under there in the mess.
With all of that junk, she never did guess.
It was way in the back,
under an old paper sack.
She hung down her head—so embarrassed.

"Seth and poor Julie!" Maddie said with a cry.
"I've been so mean." The tears filled her eyes.
"And you, Miss Missy,
my dear big sissy.
Oh, no one will ever forgive me!"

"I will," Missy said
with a smile in her eyes.
"And so will the Lord
when you apologize.
Pray to him first
when you've acted
your worst.
And then you can
talk to the others."

Maddie got down
by her bed on her knees.
She prayed to the Lord
to forgive her, please.
Her heart felt so good
and she knew that she should
go talk to her family now.

Missy went with Maddie (a sisterly favor).

Maddie said, "Sorry," and each one forgave her.

With hugs all around and the jump rope now found,

Mad Maddie was happy that day.

Mom's Moment

The Bible says in Matthew 5:23, *"If you are offering your gift at the altar and there remember that your brother has something against you, leave your gift there in front of the altar. First go and be reconciled to your brother; then come and offer your gift."*

Have you ever said something you are sorry for? We all have, whether to our child, our spouse, or someone else. Taking the leap from feeling regretful to saying "I'm sorry" is a sometimes difficult yet important step since we are models of God's love—not just to our loved ones but to the whole world.

God honors our efforts to try to be like him. Our apologies and humility honor him. He will help us and give us the strength to be the loving people we want to be.